# Sand between my Toes

illustrated by
**Jenny Duke**

written by
**Caroline Cross**

Water glistens,
I listen.

**The item should be returned or renewed by the last date stamped below.**

Dylid dychwelyd neu adnewyddu'r eitem erbyn y dyddiad olaf sydd wedi'i stampio isod.

Newport
CITY COUNCIL
CYNGOR DINAS
Casnewydd

PILLGWENLLY

To renew visit / Adnewyddwch ar
**www.newport.gov.uk/libraries**

*To Florence, who loves sea, sand,
and beaches, even when it's raining!*
**Jenny**

*To my parents and Florence,
for their unconditional love*
**Caroline**

First published in 2021 by Child's Play (International) Ltd
Ashworth Road, Bridgemead, Swindon SN5 7YD, UK

First published in USA in 2021 by Child's Play Inc
250 Minot Avenue, Auburn, Maine 04210

Distributed in Australia by Child's Play Australia Pty Ltd
Unit 10/20 Narabang Way, Belrose, Sydney, NSW 2085

Illustration copyright © 2021 Jenny Duke
Text copyright © 2021 Child's Play (International) Ltd
The moral rights of the author and illustrator have been asserted

ISBN 978-1-78628-349-8
L080221CPL05213498

Printed in Heshan, China

1 3 5 7 9 10 8 6 4 2

A catalogue record of this book
is available from the British Library

www.childs-play.com

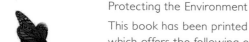

Protecting the Environment

This book has been printed using a waterless printing technique,
which offers the following environmental benefits:
No water is used in the process
No alcohol is involved, reducing greenhouse emissions
Less paper is used during set-up

Gulls cry,
dog runs by.

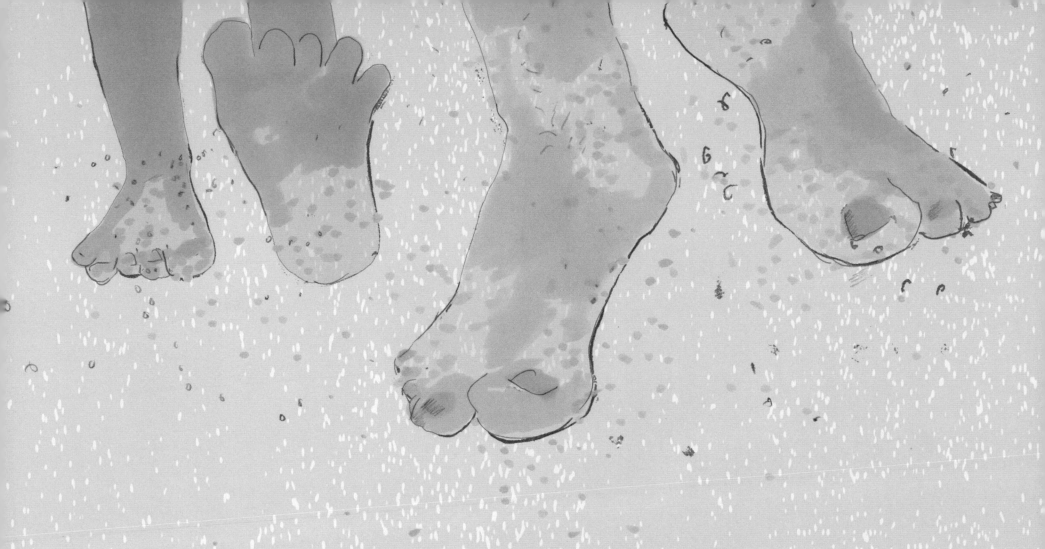

Toes wriggle, I giggle.

In the sand
I stand.

Wave crashes,

ball splashes.

Seaweed, shells,
salty smells.

Ice cream drips,

beach chair flips.

Spade clashes,

boy dashes.

Shelter rips,

bucket tips.

Damp towels,

baby howls.

Fries and sauce,

home of course.

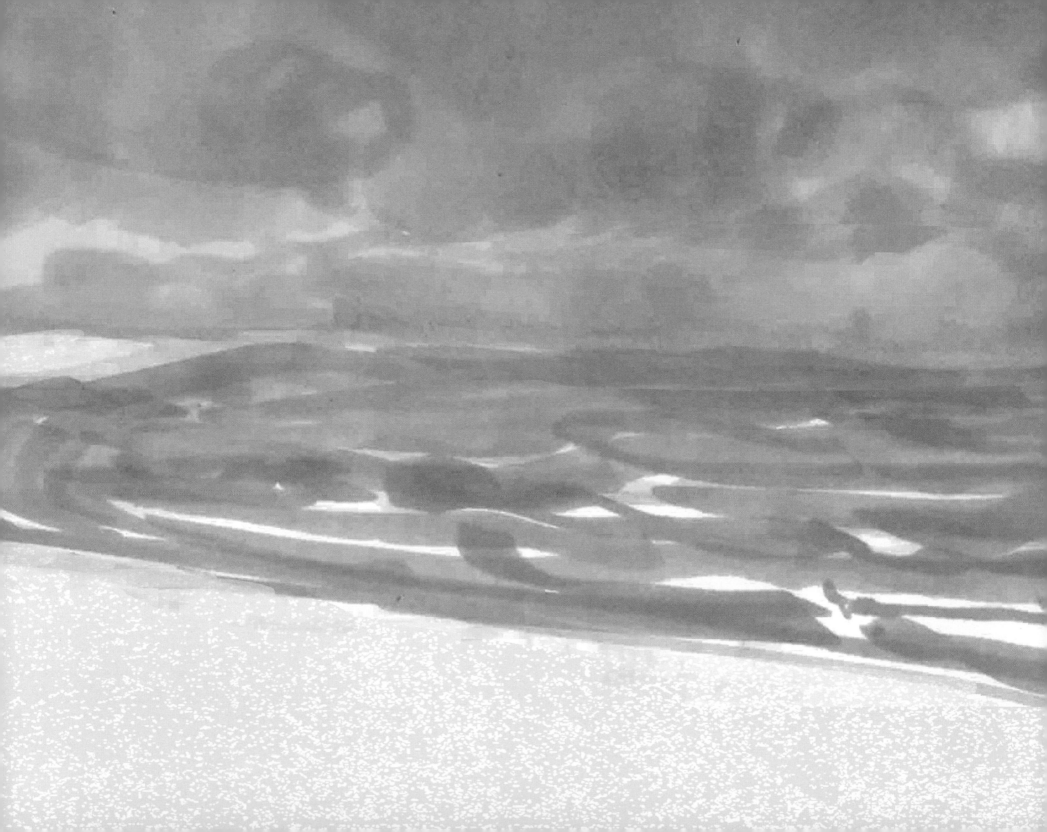

PILLGWENLLY 16/2/21